WILD CHILD

Forest's First Day of School

Forest's First Day of School

WILD CHILD

Tara Zann

[Imprint]
MAKE YOUR MARK

New York

[Imprint]
MAKE YOUR MARK

A part of Macmillan Children's Publishing Group,
a division of Macmillan Publishing Group, LLC

WILD CHILD: FOREST'S FIRST DAY OF SCHOOL. Copyright © 2017 by
Imprint. All rights reserved. Printed in the United States
of America by LSC Communications, Harrisonburg,
Virginia. For information, address Imprint,
175 Fifth Avenue, New York, N.Y. 10010.

Library of Congress Cataloging-in-Publication Data is available.
ISBN 978-1-250-10387-1 (paperback)
ISBN 978-1-250-10386-4 (ebook)

Our books may be purchased in bulk for promotional,
educational, or business use. Please contact your local
bookseller or the Macmillan Corporate and Premium Sales
Department at (800) 221-7945 ext. 5442 or by e-mail at
MacmillanSpecialMarkets@macmillan.com.

Book design by Ellen Duda
Illustrations by Dan Widdowson
Imprint logo designed by Amanda Spielman

First Edition—2017

1   3   5   7   9   10   8   6   4   2

mackids.com

To those who are wild for learning

Chapter 1

On the first day of school, Olive Regle didn't mind that her older brother, Ryan, walked ten steps ahead of her because he was too cool to walk next to his little sister. Last year it bothered her, but not this year. This year, she had someone to walk with *and* someone to keep her company: His name was Forest.

Forest dropped into Olive's life on a

camping trip. He had grown up in the forest and had no family. From the first moment Olive met him, she felt an odd bond with him. Luckily her father saw kindness in the wild Forest and let him stay and live with them. That had been only a week ago, and it had been one *crazy* week. Olive had to teach Forest how to do everything from brush his teeth to use silverware. But now there was an even bigger challenge: school.

Olive liked the learning part of school, but she didn't like feeling left out and invisible. The popular kids at school often made Olive feel like an outcast.

This year's going to be different, she thought with confidence as she walked.

She figured that since Forest was *so* different, that he would be treated as an outcast, too. Then, she and Forest would stick together, and she'd never be lonely at school anymore. In fact, Olive thought it felt nice to be excited to go to school— for a change.

Olive looked over at Forest, who was wearing his backpack on the front of his body as if it were a frontpack.

They turned right at Blackstock Way and left at Pine Street. A large playground

came into view. Olive smiled as she watched Forest's eyes grow wide. Before this, his jungle gym was the forest itself, so this was a whole new thing to him.

"Come on, Forest," said Olive, tugging him away. "We'll come out here later for recess."

"What's 'recess'?" asked Forest.

"It's when we get to leave the classroom and run around on the playground," explained Olive.

"Oh . . ." said Forest.

Beyond the playground were basketball hoops and a large field. Olive steered Forest away from the playground and toward a group of buildings to the left. They were all one story with a big number on each one of them, with brightly painted doors that opened to the outside.

This year, Olive and Forest's third-grade class was in Room 7. As the pair entered the room, the teacher spoke up.

"Please find your name on the correct desk and then have a seat," said Mrs. Finn.

Olive was relieved to see that her desk and Forest's desk were right next to each other. She took her seat and pointed to where Forest should sit. Around them, kids were either already sitting in their seats or standing near them and talking. For a split second, Olive felt a pang of

loneliness. Then she remembered that she had Forest on her side and smiled as she looked over at him.

That's when Josie Letay walked into the classroom, laughing loudly with her friends. Olive frowned and turned away. Josie Letay was the most popular girl in her class every single year. Even in kindergarten she was popular! Josie was noisy and funny, with lots of friends. Olive, on the other hand, had always been shy and quiet—and alone.

At that moment, Mrs. Finn approached Olive's desk. Olive felt a little nervous, and looked down. "You must be Ryan Regle's sister. He was in my class two years ago," said Mrs. Finn in a stern voice.

"But I'm nothing like him," Olive said quickly.

"That's good," said Mrs. Finn, her eyebrows arched up. "Let's keep it that way."

Olive looked over, about to say something to Forest, but he wasn't at his desk. She scanned the room and found him by the class pet: a fat little fur ball of a hamster.

Well, of course he found the animal in here, thought Olive with a smile. Not only was Forest drawn to animals, he had the ability to communicate with them. It was amazing to see him chittering with squirrels or barking at her dog.

Olive was about to go and check out the hamster, too, when the bell rang. *RIIIING!!!!*

That's when Olive realized she forgot to warn Forest about the bells! She could see Forest's mass of hair flipping wildly as he looked around, trying to figure

out the source of the ringing sound. Olive cringed as Forest leaped up on a desk and screeched at the top of his voice. All the other kids covered their ears.

"The bell just means to sit down in your chair," Olive explained.

"Okay," said Forest, climbing back down and sitting in his seat. "I'll talk to Bell later?"

Olive opened her mouth to correct Forest's plan of having a chat with the school bell when Mrs. Finn clapped her hands to get everyone's attention. "Welcome to the third grade," she began. "I think it's going to be a great year. First, I'd like to introduce a new student to our school. He's had a very unusual upbringing. He grew up among the redwood trees. Would you please come up here, Forest?"

Uh-oh, thought Olive. *What on earth is Forest going to say?*

Chapter 2

Looking unsure but following Mrs. Finn's encouragement, Forest walked slowly to the front of the room. Mrs. Finn signaled that he should turn around to face the class. Forest looked at Mrs. Finn with a look that said, *Now what do I do?*

"Why don't you tell us a little about yourself?" suggested Mrs. Finn.

"Uh . . ." said Forest.

He looked over the sea of unfamiliar

faces. He'd never been looked at by so many people at once. He didn't want to disappoint Olive, but Forest had absolutely no idea what he was supposed to say!

Mrs. Finn could tell that Forest was uncomfortable, so she tried something different. "Forest, why don't you tell us something you like or like doing?"

Forest thought for a moment. Then his eye caught something across the room—the hamster.

"Forest likes animals," he said proudly. "Forest can talk to animals."

"Oh, really?" said Mrs. Finn, thinking Forest was just playing.

"Yes," insisted Forest. "The hamster over there wants a bigger cage with a wheel and a fountain and . . . what is a 'piano'?"

Mrs. Finn laughed uncomfortably. "Well, you certainly have quite an imagination, Forest! I'm sure that Henrietta the Hamster is perfectly happy in her current home."

"Oh, no," said Forest. "Henrietta is boy hamster! His real name is . . . ," and Forest made a little squeaking sound.

Some of the kids laughed and tried making the sound themselves.

"Thank you, Forest, for that . . . uh . . . informative speech," said Mrs. Finn. "Will you please take your seat?"

Forest walked over to his desk and with a heave, lifted it up. "Where should Forest take seat? Here?" He swung his seat around, banging into the desks next to him. "Or over here?" He banged into the desks on the other side.

The class giggled. Olive shook her head.

"I mean sit down," said Mrs. Finn.

"Oh," said Forest. He sat down.

"I mean, sit down in your *chair*," said Mrs. Finn. "Not on the floor."

"Why Mrs. Finn not say that before?" said Forest as he sat down at his desk. "So confusing!"

"I . . . never mind," said Mrs. Finn. She turned toward the whiteboard and began writing. "Class, I'd like you to take out a—" She turned back around. "Forest, why are you standing on Olive's desk?"

"Forest protect Olive from strange flying objects."

"That's a paper airplane, Forest," whispered Olive, catching one.

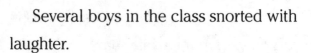

Several boys in the class snorted with laughter.

"Forest, please sit down," said Mrs. Finn. "In your *seat*. Then stay there."

He sat. He stayed.

Once Forest was seated, Mrs. Finn handed out pieces of paper. "Everyone, please take out a pencil and write down three things you did this summer."

Olive took out a pencil from her pencil case and motioned for Forest to do the same. Forest opened his case and looked at the pencils, which looked like yellow twigs to him. He took out two of the pencils and rubbed them together, hoping to start a fire. Olive reached over and stopped him.

"Psst!" said Olive. "You write like this," she said to Forest.

He watched her write, smiled, and tried it himself.

Crack! Forest's pencil broke in half. He quickly began using the other one. A few seconds later . . . *crack!* Another broken pencil. He was pressing down way too hard. The paper he was using had tons of tears in it, as well.

After seven more broken pencils and bits of paper flying about, Mrs. Finn came over. "Forest," she said, arching an eyebrow, "what do you think you're doing?"

"Forest writing," he said, furrowing his brow in concentration.

"Mrs. Finn," Olive offered quietly, "I don't think Forest has ever used a pencil and paper before. Sticks and mud were more his style, I think."

"No," said Forest. "Carve on tree trunks. Oh!" His face brightened. "Forest could carve desk!"

"There will be no carving on desk-tops in this classroom!" Mrs. Finn insisted.

"Okay," said Forest. "Forest take desk outside for carving!"

"Stop picking up your desk!" yelled Mrs. Finn. "Sit down! Please!"

Forest slowly eased down the desk and sat. As Mrs. Finn stomped back up to the front of the classroom, Forest leaned over to Olive.

"Why Olive banging her head on desk?"

Chapter 3

When the bell rang for recess, all the kids rushed out of the classroom.

"What's happening?" Forest asked Olive.

"It's time for recess," Olive said. "We get to go outside."

"Forever?" asked Forest.

Olive smiled. "No. Just for twenty minutes."

When Forest frowned, Olive added,

"But we can go play on the big playground."

That made Forest happy. Like a bolt of lightning, he ran ahead to get there first. By the time Olive made it to the playground, she heard a bunch of clapping. A large group of kids surrounded Forest, who was doing some pretty crazy tricks on the monkey bars, swinging and leaping from one to the other. Olive tried to get Forest's attention, but he didn't see her. He was too busy investigating something he'd never seen before: swings. Not knowing how to use them, he just climbed up the chain of the swing to the top and swung around the horizontal bar at the top, doing one loop the loop after another.

When he landed, the kids rushed over to him and all spoke at once: "That was so cool! Where did you learn how to do that? Can you teach me how to do that?"

But Olive didn't rush over. She hung back, feeling weird. She thought that Forest growing up in the forest would make him an outcast, and then it would just be she and Forest against the world. But to her surprise, the other kids thought Forest was super cool. They wanted to hear all about his adventures living in the wild.

"Did you really live in the woods?"

"Forest, what was it like living in a super-tall tree?"

"How did you not fall out when you were asleep?"

"Did you just eat nuts and berries?"

"Did you ever meet a bear?"

"Did you eat bugs?"

"Did you ever meet a platypus?"

Olive rolled her eyes. Jason McDoodle always asked the silliest questions. Olive watched Forest looking dazzled by all the attention, and her shoulders slumped. She turned to go sit down on a bench when she heard Forest calling her name. She spun around, hopeful.

Finally! she thought.

"Olive play, too?" asked Forest.

Olive was about to stand up and say yes, but before she could, Josie Letay stepped in front of her.

"Olive doesn't play," said Josie with a shrug. "She just sits there like a bump on a log, her nose buried in some book."

"Olive buries nose?" asked Forest, his head tilted in confusion.

"Come on," said Josie, taking Forest's arm. "I'll show you how to play tag."

They walked away together, and Olive sat there, all alone.

***

When the bell rang, signaling recess was over, Olive noticed that Forest still jumped a little in surprise. He also tried to make the bell sound again. She walked toward him, but someone got there first.

"Hey, Forest," said Robbie Ipswitch. "I'll race you back to class!"

The boys zoomed off, leaving Olive standing alone, again, on the playground. She sighed and walked back to class by herself.

Once Olive was back at her desk, and class had started, Forest tried to get her attention. But she ignored him; her feelings were hurt. So she kept her eyes straight ahead and Forest was forced to say "Olive! Olive! *Olive!* OLIVE!" until Mrs. Finn made him stop.

Mrs. Finn addressed the class. "Please finish up your assignment about what you did over the summer," she said. Then

she busied herself with some papers at her desk.

Olive was about to get to work when she noticed Forest wasn't in his seat. Eyes wide with dread, she looked around the classroom. Where did he go?

Jason McDoodle saw Olive looking around and pointed to the classroom's open window.

Olive's mouth dropped open as Forest's smiling head popped up outside the window.

Silent as a cat, Forest climbed back in the window. Olive wasn't sure what surprised her more: that Forest had left and come back without the teacher noticing, or that no one was tattling on him.

It wasn't until Forest sat down that

Olive saw a big scoop of mud in his hands. He plopped it on his desk with a *splut*!

Mrs. Finn, with a teacher's instinct for Sounds That Do Not Belong in the Classroom, finally looked up. Her eyes grew wide on seeing the mound of mud on Forest's desk.

"Forest," she said, as calmly as she could, "what are you doing?"

"The assignment," said Forest. "Forest write out what he did last summer." He immediately began to draw pictures in the mud.

"Here Forest have acorn fight with squirrels," he said. "And here Forest climb highest tree!"

"We do *not* use mud to write—"

"Forest finish assignment?"

"Yes! Fine! Just clean it up!"

"Can I do my next assignment in mud, too?" asked Jason McDoodle.

"No! No mud!" declared Mrs. Finn.

The class gave a big "Awww."

Meanwhile, Forest had filled a bucket with water from the classroom sink and upended the entire thing all over his desk, splashing water and mud on everyone around him, including Mrs. Finn.

"Desk all clean!" said Forest happily.

Mrs. Finn made a little scratchy sound from deep in her throat that Olive thought sort of sounded like a growl.

After Olive taught Forest how to clean up properly with lots and lots of paper towels, the class finally calmed down a little. Mrs. Finn wiped her hands and prepared to begin teaching again. She went to the board.

"Boys and girls," began Mrs. Finn, "we're going to start our unit on ancient Egypt. The ancient Egyptians wrote using an alphabet made of little pictures, called hieroglyphs, instead of letters. I'll draw some examples on the board for you." She turned around and began drawing on the board.

"What's that?" Forest asked aloud. He

pointed to one of Mrs. Finn's drawings. "Very sick duck?"

Snorts and giggles rippled through the classroom. Even Olive laughed.

"Please raise your hand before speaking," Mrs. Finn said to Forest. "And it's an

ibis, not a duck. Now, these three hiero-glyphs represent the letters M, A, and—"

"I've never seen a duck ibis before," said Forest.

Mrs. Finn sighed. "Forest, I asked you to raise your hand before speaking."

"Forest did! Look!" Forest pointed to his left hand, which hovered about an inch above the surface of his desk. "Forest's hand is raised."

"I meant raise it in the air," said Mrs. Finn. "Like this!"

"Oh," said Forest.

"You understand now?"

Forest nodded.

"Good. Now, as I was saying, these three hieroglyphs represent—"

"Hey, Olive!" Forest yelled. "Do you have any food?"

"Forest!" shouted Mrs. Finn.

"What?" asked Forest. "Forest's hand raised. Look! All the way up, like you showed." Sure enough, his hand was straight up as he talked. A puzzled look crossed his face. "But you speak without raising *your* hand. Can you raise hand, please, Mrs. Finn?"

More laughter echoed throughout the room.

"I am the teacher," said Mrs. Finn

through clenched teeth. "I don't have to raise my hand. You do. And when you do, you stay quiet until I call on you. Then, *and only then*, can you speak."

"Oh," said Forest. "Okay."

"Got it?" asked Mrs. Finn.

"Got it."

"Good. Great. Glad to hear it." Mrs. Finn cleared her throat. "The Egyptian hieroglyphs . . . Forest?"

"Yes?"

"You're raising your hand," said Mrs. Finn.

"Yes!" he said.

"Do you have a question?" she asked.

"Yes!"

"What is it?"

"Olive!" asked Forest. "Do you have any food?"

The class erupted in laughter.

Chapter
4

Lunchtime arrived shortly after noon.
Normally, Olive hated lunchtime even
more than PE (and she *despised* PE). She
always sat alone and read a book. But
today, Forest was by her side again. He
had apologized for not playing with her
at recess. Olive was happy to have her
friend back! She steered him to the back
of the cafeteria line and grabbed a tray.
Up ahead, on the other side of a counter,

Mrs. Snagglebaum, the grouchy lunch lady, served each student.

"What is that?" asked Forest, pointing to the lunches. "Exploded rat?"

"No, that's . . ." Olive leaned in to look closer, "spaghetti with meatballs. Possibly. I hope so, anyway. I'm really hungry."

"Me, too," said Forest. "Forest get us food."

Not understanding the idea of waiting your turn, Forest jumped on the counter. He picked up a plate and reached for a meatball to give to Olive.

"Ouch!" said Forest. It was hotter than he expected.

"Hey! What do you think you're doing?!" said the lunch lady in a low, scratchy voice. She pointed her serving spoon at him.

"Getting lunch!" said Forest, much to the amusement of the other kids in line. Then he squatted down, grabbed the serving spoon, used it to scoop some meatballs and spaghetti on a plate, and handed the plate to Olive. He spotted some round rolls on the counter, as well.

"Catch!" Forest said to Olive.

"Forest, you shouldn't—"

As she caught the flying roll, all the kids around her suddenly wanted to join in.

"Me, too! Me, too! Throw one to me, Forest!" they chanted.

Forest was only too happy to throw rolls left, right, and center.

But one person was *not* happy with the airborne food: Mrs. Snagglebaum. "Stop that right now, you little hooligan!" She lunged at Forest, but he was far too fast to get caught in her clutches.

Forest dropped the serving spoon and ran around to the other side of the counter. Looking over his shoulder, he could see Mrs. Snagglebaum chasing him, her doughy face twisted and red from the supreme effort of running several yards. She'd grabbed her serving spoon and shook it at him, flinging tomato sauce all over herself and several nearby

students. Forest bolted across the cafeteria and jumped up onto a table to escape.

"Get down here!" bellowed the lunch lady.

"Never!" cried Forest. He looked down and saw some spaghetti and meatballs on another student's plate. He stood up defiantly on the table.

"Get down here NOW!" shrieked the lunch lady. Her face was so red Olive was afraid the woman was going to have a heart attack. "I'm taking you to the principal!"

Of course Forest didn't know what that meant. So he just threw two meatballs at her. They landed exactly in the middle of her forehead. This surprised Mrs. Snagglebaum so much that she

began to fall backward. She windmilled her arms to try to regain balance, but only managed to slap the lunch tray out of Sheldon Fickle's hands. The very full tray of food landed all over Olive.

"Ew! Gross!" cried Olive.

Mrs. Snagglebaum toppled over, only barely avoiding squishing some of the students. Meanwhile, the kids in the cafeteria didn't need any prodding to get involved: Half of them smeared food

on their own faces, and several jumped on Forest's table to join him.

"Follow Forest!" cried Josie, her own face decorated with sauce.

Furious, Mrs. Snagglebaum rolled over and got up. Moving with surprising speed, she grabbed Forest's ankle.

"GOT YOU!"

She let go when he howled, exactly like a wolf. Not a kid pretending to howl like a wolf, but sounding precisely like a

long-toothed carnivore on a cold forest night. Forest wasn't howling because he was scared. He howled to bring his pack to him.

The kids in the cafeteria, already feeling a little like wild animals, heeded the cry without thinking. They howled, too. The battle was on!

Everyone was quickly pelted with meatballs and slimed with spaghetti.

Olive was about to go hide under a table when she saw Mrs. Snagglebaum lurching toward her, trying to escape the barrage of meatballs and spaghetti. But the lunch lady was already so covered with oily tomato sauce that she slipped on the slick floor directly in front of Olive, making Olive yelp.

"STOP THIS AT *ONCE!*" commanded a voice over a bullhorn. "EVERYONE STEP AWAY FROM THE MEATBALLS! NOW!"

The students stopped moving and turned to see the principal, Dr. Poole, looking extremely angry. Next to him stood Mrs. Finn, shock and horror spread across her face. All around them, limp spaghetti dripped from the walls, ceilings, and light fixtures. Red sauce was splattered all over the floor, walls, and children. One chunky bit dripped from the ceiling and landed on Mrs. Finn's head with a gentle *splut.*

"YOU WILL CLEAN YOURSELVES UP AND REPORT BACK HERE—IMMEDIATELY!" announced the principal.

Heads hanging down, the kids filed out of the cafeteria and into the bathrooms. Once they'd washed most of the food off their hands, picked spaghetti noodles out of their hair, and were generally clean, they returned to the cafeteria.

"What has gotten into you?" Mrs. Finn said to her class. "I'm very disappointed in you."

Forest raised his hand. "I'm still hungry."

"Then you shouldn't have wasted food by throwing it!"

"Forest no waste food," said Forest. "Food still good. Just on floor. Forest has eaten worse."

"I don't doubt that for a minute," said Mrs. Finn, shaking her head. She addressed the class. "Well, instead of doing the fun art project I planned for this afternoon, you will all stay here and clean up the entire cafeteria. You will scrub every nook. You will rinse every cranny."

She glared at the children and then continued. "An adult will check to make sure you're doing a good job." She turned to the clearly furious lunch lady.

"Mrs. Snagglebaum, they're all yours."
The lunch lady smiled.
Olive gulped.

Chapter
5

By Friday afternoon, the students were definitely ready for the upcoming weekend. Everyone had made it through the first week of school, despite the cafeteria chaos and cleanup.

Mrs. Finn stood in front of the class. "It's been a very long and uh . . . interesting . . . week," she began, with a pointed look at Forest.

Forest didn't understand what she really meant and said, "Thank you!"

Josie Letay giggled. "He's so funny," she whispered to Mara Doyle.

Barf, thought Olive.

Mrs. Finn cleared her throat. "Listen up. I have an exciting announcement."

This perked everyone up. They looked at one another curiously and leaned forward in their chairs, eager to hear the news. Olive tried to imagine what it could be: A new class pet? A field trip to Mars? Sending the class pet on a field trip to Mars?

"Our third grade class will be rehearsing and performing a show this fall," said Mrs. Finn.

Blech, thought Olive.

"Cool!" said Josie, who was no stranger to acting.

Olive imagined Josie spending hours in front of her mirror at home practicing being famous and adored by millions.

"What show is it?" asked Josie, raising her hand.

"A version of *The Wizard of Oz*," said Mrs. Finn.

"Wow! That's going to be awesome!" said Lola Figueroa.

"Can I play Dorothy?" asked Grace O'Donnelly.

"Maybe you should be Toto instead!" joked Jason McDoodle.

Grace playfully pushed him. "Maybe *you* should!"

"Now," continued Mrs. Finn, "first

there will be tryouts where you will have to audition for the roles in the show."

Olive frowned. She didn't want to be in the play *at all*. In fact, she couldn't think of a worse thing to have to do. Except smell her brother's stinky feet. Or be stuck in a car with Josie for twenty-four hours.

Then she brightened. *I know! I'll just not audition. Problem solved! Hurray!* She was quite happy with this new plan until . . .

Mrs. Finn said: "*Everyone* has to audition and *everyone* will be cast in the show."

Problem NOT *solved!* thought Olive. *Ugh!*

Eric Keizer raised his hand.

"Yes, Eric?" said Mrs. Finn.

"I have tuba lessons after school, so I won't be able to make rehearsals," said Eric. He tried to look especially earnest. "I am *so* sorry I'll miss it."

Oh, man! thought Olive. *I wish I had tuba practice! Then I'd get out of rehearsals, too!*

Mrs. Finn smiled knowingly. "Well, rest assured that you will not miss any of your tuba lessons, Eric. Rehearsals will be during school hours."

"Drat!" said Eric under his breath.

Drat! thought Olive.

"Tryouts are next week, so start thinking about what role you want to audition for," said Mrs. Finn as the bell rang. "Have a nice weekend!"

***

As Olive and Forest walked home that afternoon, Olive dragged her feet. "I don't want to be in the show."

"What *is* a show?" asked Forest.

"It's where you pretend to be someone else on a stage," explained Olive. "You tell a story, and sometimes there's singing and dancing. There are costumes and makeup and sets and lights. All together, it makes up a show."

"Sounds fun!" said Forest.

"What?! I think it sounds *awful*," replied Olive. "All those people staring up at you?"

Forest's face turned serious. "Forest spend whole life in trees so people *not* see him. Hiding, running, sneaking, no talk, no laughing. Made Forest lonely."

Olive gently put her hand on his shoulder.

"But Forest come here and sees everyone. And everyone sees Forest," he said. "And it's fun. Forest loves to tell stories and hear stories."

"Well, yes, but—"

"Is Wibbarg of Odd a good story?" asked Forest.

"*Wizard of Oz*," corrected Olive. "Yes, it's a good story."

"Then show will be fun!" insisted Forest.

Olive thought about what Forest said and how convinced he was that the show was a good idea.

"Maybe you're right, Forest," she said. "Maybe it will be fun."

And that's how Olive and Forest ended up spending the entire weekend practicing for the auditions. Olive even started to think it would be really exciting to play

Dorothy. A girl in a strange new place, figuring it out as she goes along. It reminded Olive of what Forest was doing at school every day. He was also in a strange new place, figuring it out.

Then late Sunday night, when Olive was in bed, she started to get nervous. She had been having so much fun practicing with Forest all weekend, she forgot one possible problem: Josie Letay. How would Olive ever win the lead role with Josie trying out?

Chapter 6

On the day of the tryouts, Olive woke up feeling jittery and nervous. Her father had called that feeling "butterflies in your stomach," but Olive was so anxious it felt like a few big lizards were running around in there, too. Olive tried to not let it bother her too much. She almost succeeded. While she got dressed, she tried really hard to clamp down on her nerves about

Josie and tried to remember what Forest said: It should be fun.

As she and Forest walked to school, Olive found that she was actually excited!

Maybe I'll even get a better part than Josie, she thought to herself.

Auditions began right after lunch. The whole class walked over to the school's auditorium. The play would be performed on the stage inside. Mrs. Finn sat down in the audience, with clipboard and pen at the ready. She asked all the girls trying out for the role of Dorothy to go backstage.

"I will call you when it is your turn," said Mrs. Finn. "Then please come out and stand on the blue T in the middle of the stage." She scanned the list of names from the sign-up sheets and called out the first person: Katie Johnson.

Katie walked out onstage to the T made of blue tape. In front of her, she held a piece of paper with the lines she needed to read aloud, but she seemed to be holding it really, really, *really* close to her face.

"Katie, please put the page down. We have to see your face," said Mrs. Finn. "Straight back, shoulders broad, and face the audience. Then, project! They should hear you in the back row. Ready?"

Katie put the page down by her waist and looked down at it. She squinted and her hair fell over her face.

"I . . . uh . . . forgot my glasses," said Katie.

"Well, just do your best," said Mrs. Finn.

She was supposed to say: "Come along, Toto. We will go to the Emerald City and ask the Great Oz how to get back to Kansas again."

But Katie couldn't make out any of the words on the page; it was just too blurry. She tried . . .

"Hey, Toto, let's go to the Emerald Monkey and ask the great Kansas how to get back home to Oz."

Backstage, Olive could hear Josie snickering to her friends. "Katie should have pretended to be sick today and stayed home."

"I think *I* might be sick from listening to her!" joked Mara.

"Ha! Good one!" Emily Harper said with a high five.

"Why do you have to be so mean?" Olive said under her breath.

Josie whirled around. "What was that?"

Olive's face flushed. She looked down at her shoes. "Nothing."

Just then, Mrs. Finn called Josie to

the stage. It was her turn to audition. Before going, Josie smirked and said, "Watch and learn, girls." With that, Josie strode onto the stage like she owned it.

Of course, she did a great job on her audition.

"Thank you, Josie, that was excellent," said Mrs. Finn.

Josie flashed a huge smile and walked off the stage, proud as a peacock. "Told you I'd be amazing," she announced to everyone within earshot.

Olive groaned.

"Is there a problem?" Josie asked Olive.

Olive felt her throat dry up, wishing she could come up with a clever response. But nothing came to mind.

"Olive!" called Mrs. Finn from the audience.

Josie put her hands on her hips. "Good luck, superstar."

Olive slowly made her way onstage. After the exchange with Josie, she felt nervous and shy. She heard Forest in the audience cheering her on, but it didn't help. Olive stood on the blue T onstage and opened her mouth, but nothing came out.

"Uh, can you please speak up?" Mrs. Finn called.

Olive opened and closed her mouth, but not a single sound escaped. It was like her lungs had turned to stone.

"Louder, please!" said Mrs. Finn, clearly annoyed.

Olive tried to push out a sound, but

only managed a pitiful little squeak. She could imagine Josie and her friends laughing backstage. Trying to hold back tears, Olive ran off the stage.

When she made it to where Forest was sitting in audience, she plopped down next to him. "That was horrible," she groaned.

"Not horrible," said Forest. "Just very, very quiet. Next one better."

"No way. I can't try out for anything else," Olive insisted. "I'm too embarrassed."

"Forest sorry Olive feel sad," he said.

Olive looked over at him. "Thanks, Forest. Maybe I was just fooling myself that I could get a good part in the show."

"Forest!" called Mrs. Finn. "Please come to the stage. It's your turn."

Instead of climbing the few stairs to the stage, Forest jumped onto it in one leap. He walked to the blue T and turned around.

"Forest not be Dorothy," he said, shaking his head back and forth emphatically.

Mrs. Finn smiled. "I realize that," she

said. "Did you want to try for another part?"

"Olive told me about play," said Forest. "No lion for me. Lion not brave at all."

"Maybe the scarecrow, then?" asked Mrs. Finn.

"No. Crows really like Forest. Not scared of him."

"Hmm. How about one of the flying monkeys?" suggested Mrs. Finn.

"Monkey? What is monkey?" asked Forest.

In the audience, Olive smacked her forehead, realizing she forgot to tell him about the monkeys in the show.

Of course he wouldn't have seen one where he used to live, she thought.

"A monkey is a creature with a long

tail that can climb trees and jump from branch to branch," explained Mrs. Finn.

"And fly?" asked Forest.

"Not in real life," said Mrs. Finn. "Just in the show. There are wings on their backs."

"Like birds?"

Mrs. Finn shifted in her seat. "Well, yes, sort of."

"Then why not have birds in show? Why monkeys?" asked Forest.

"Because that's what the author wrote," explained Mrs. Finn, starting to

lose her patience. "He wanted flying monkeys."

"Why?" asked Forest. "Are flying monkeys better than birds?"

"There's no such thing as flying monkeys!"

"So monkeys not real?"

"Monkeys are real! They don't fly! They only fly in the story. Flying monkeys are made-up!" said Mrs. Finn.

"Forest not understand," he said.

"That's fine," said Mrs. Finn. "It doesn't matter. We'll deal with it later. Just make a sound like a monkey for your audition, okay? I still have a lot of other kids to get through."

"Okay," said Forest.

"Great," said Mrs. Finn. "Fine. Good. Go ahead."

She waited. There was silence.

"Well?" she asked.

"Forest never hear monkey before. What sound they make?"

Mrs. Finn sighed deeply.

Josie skipped back out onstage and showed Forest her phone, playing a clip of a nature show about monkeys.

"Oh, I see," said Forest. "Monkeys made sound like this." He opened his mouth and made a very good, and very loud, copy of the sound he'd just heard.

After Mrs. Finn and the other children removed their hands from their ears, Mrs. Finn said, "That was remarkably . . . accurate, Forest. Very good. And thank you for your help, Josie, but perhaps

howler monkeys was not the most perfect choice."

"WHAT DID YOU SAY?" yelled Josie, her ears still ringing.

Chapter 7

On Wednesday, Olive and Forest arrived at school to see a bunch of kids gathered around the front door of the classroom.

"What's going on?" Olive asked Katie.

"The cast list has been posted," replied Katie.

Olive made her way to the front and scanned the list.

"Look, Forest, you get to be a flying monkey!" said Olive.

Forest's eyes opened wide. "For real?"

"No, no. Just for pretend. You get to pretend to be one."

"Oh," said Forest.

Then Olive looked for her own name. It was at the very bottom . . . under the role of a "tree." She was just a part of the scenery.

Then Olive looked at the rest of the cast list, and her shoulders slumped. She quickly recovered as she heard Josie's voice behind her.

"Congratulations," Josie said to Forest. "Looks like we're going to be spending a lot of time together."

Forest just shrugged. But Olive narrowed her eyes at Josie, knowing the game she was playing. As she turned away from the list, she whispered to Forest, "Well, it's not surprising to see Josie cast as the Wicked Witch. No acting going on there, I suppose."

Unfortunately, Josie heard. Her cheeks were red, making Olive feel a little bad about what she'd said. "Ha. Ha. Ha," replied Josie in a monotone. "You're so clever—*for a tree!*" She huffed and walked

away, Olive's moment of guilt disappearing with her.

I wish I WERE a tree, thought Olive. *I'd drop a branch right on your head.*

Olive walked to her desk and sat down, wondering what kind of tree costume would be the best for covering her completely from head to toe.

***

Over the next few weeks, Mrs. Finn scheduled rehearsals three days a week. Olive dreaded those days. It would often consist of her sitting in the audience, bored to tears, or worse: being onstage as a tree, with her arms held up in uncomfortable positions.

Josie would then "accidentally" bump into Olive. "Oh! Olive!" she would say. "I

didn't see you there. You're *sooo* good at fading into the background."

Olive, as usual, said nothing.

One Wednesday during rehearsal, Josie and Forest were learning a scene where the witch looks into her crystal ball, spying on Dorothy and her friends. Forest, as Josie's flying monkey, was supposed to be looking, too.

"Look, my pet," said Josie in her best witch voice. "The wretched little girl and her foolish friends are—"

Forest picked up the crystal ball, which was an empty milk jug because the crystal ball prop hadn't been made yet.

"Forest not see little girl."

The entire cast groaned.

"Forest!" said Josie.

"It's pretend, Forest, remember? It's

acting," said Mrs. Finn. "Just look at the milk jug and don't say anything."

"But Forest do it that way *last* time," he complained.

"Yes," said Mrs. Finn. "That's good. Please do it the same way every time."

"That boring. Forest want to do it different! I can be flying cow next time?"

"No, Forest," Mrs. Finn said louder. "You are a flying monkey, not a flying cow or dog or toaster or chair. You will shuffle around on your monkey legs, look into the crystal ball, and nod your monkey head, okay? Monkeys don't talk."

"Monkeys not fly, either," observed Forest.

"It's made up!" barked Mrs. Finn. "You're in the magical land of Oz, you work for a green witch because that's the only job a flying monkey can get, and you *don't talk*! Got it?!"

Forest was silent.

"I said, got—"

"You said no talk," said Forest.

Wow, thought Olive. Mrs. Finn's left eye was really twitching, and Olive thought she could hear her teeth grinding from across the theater.

"Let's keep going," Mrs. Finn announced. "Or we'll never get past this scene."

Josie cleared her throat and looked into the crystal milk jug. "The slippers!" she cackled. "I must have those slippers!"

At that moment, Forest stood up and walked into the audience and over to Celine Filibuster, the girl playing Dorothy. Forest bent down and plucked off her shoes. He returned to the stage.

"Oo, oo! Ee, ee!" said Forest, imitating a monkey as he handed the "slippers" to Josie the witch.

The entire cast groaned again.

"Mrs. Finn!" said Josie. "I can't work like this! I'll be in my trailer!"

"You don't have a trailer," said Mrs. Finn to Josie, who was too busy stomping off the stage to remember that she wasn't actually a movie star.

With a sigh, Mrs. Finn turned to Olive.

"Olive, dear, I have a Very Important Assignment for you."

"Yes, Mrs. Finn?" said Olive, excited. Maybe she'd have some lines or change her part or . . . ?

"Can you rehearse with Forest every single day at home? He's really got to understand how this acting thing works, and I don't have enough time to teach

him—I have a whole play to direct. Can you help me with that? Please?"

"Yes, Mrs. Finn," said Olive, her small hope crushed.

"That's a good girl," said Mrs. Finn. "Now I've got to go calm down Josie. She's really turning into the star of the show, so we'll have to put up with a little drama."

I think I've had about as much drama as I can handle, thought Olive.

Chapter 8

Day after day, Olive rehearsed at home after school with Forest. She played the Wicked Witch and read all her lines. She continually reminded Forest where to go and to not say a word. She also showed him pictures and videos of monkeys.

Forest appeared to understand what he was supposed to do, but Olive wasn't completely convinced. She felt like she

was trying to train an easily distracted puppy. Would he do the right thing when it was showtime?

When opening night finally arrived, backstage buzzed with activity, and Mrs. Finn flitted around like a crazy hummingbird from one kid to the next, making sure costumes were right, makeup was applied, and everyone knew their cues.

Meanwhile, Olive stood in front of one of the makeup mirrors applying her stage makeup. Other trees were taller, so their eye shadow and blush were wood-brown, but Olive was playing more of a shrub, so hers was leaf-green. Her face stuck through a hole in the costume, though Olive didn't know why the costume designer bothered. It's not like she moved or had any

lines to speak. Looking in the mirror, she saw that Josie had just walked in. Olive took a deep breath, readying herself for the "Josie" show.

But that didn't happen. That's when Olive noticed that Josie didn't look confident or smug or really anything like she usually did. Instead, Josie looked worried. Olive spun around in her chair to

see what was going on. Forest was curious, too.

"Lost . . . my . . . voice," Josie managed to squeak out. She sounded like a hundred-year-old frog.

"YOU WHAT?" yelled Mrs. Finn, surprising everyone. "I, uh, mean, how did you lose your voice?"

Mara Doyle, standing next to Josie, explained: "She went to a synchronized swimming competition yesterday to cheer on her grandmother. I think she cheered a bit too much."

"Well, this is terrible!" fussed Mrs. Finn. "A Wicked Witch without a voice isn't very scary. What are we going to do?"

"She could mime!" said someone.

"Absolutely not," said Mrs. Finn. She

peeked out into the audience and saw that almost every seat was taken.

Olive looked at the clock. The curtain was supposed to go up in five minutes. She could hear the audience getting restless.

Forest tapped Mrs. Finn on the shoulder.

"Not now, Forest," said Mrs. Finn.

He tapped again. "Forest have idea," he said.

"I don't have time right now; I have to find a new Wicked Witch," said Mrs. Finn.

"Forest knows!"

"Well, if you know, then let me figure it out," said Mrs. Finn.

"No," said Forest.

"No?" repeated a surprised Mrs. Finn.

"No. Forest knows good witch."

"I don't need a good witch," said Mrs. Finn. "I need a wicked witch."

"Olive be Wicked Witch!" said Forest.

"Hey!" said Olive. "That's not nice!"

"No! Uh . . . Olive *play* Wicked Witch," said Forest.

"Oh!" exclaimed Mrs. Finn. "What a wonderful idea!"

But when Mrs. Finn turned to her, Olive was shaking her head.

"Wait . . . no . . . I couldn't," she stammered.

"Why not?" asked Forest. "You already have green makeup!"

"Yes, you do," echoed Mrs. Finn. "You know all the lines, from practicing with Forest, right?"

"That's true, but . . ." began Olive. She pulled Forest aside. "I don't want all those people looking at me."

Forest put a comforting hand on Olive's shoulder. "Olive not being Olive onstage. Olive playing Wicked Witch. Like you tell Forest: It's acting."

"Did I say that?" asked Olive.

Forest nodded and smiled.

"Darn," said Olive. "You're right, but I'm still scared."

Mrs. Finn began flitting around again. "Can you fit in Josie's costume? JOSIE, WHERE ARE YOU? I NEED YOUR COSTUME! Okay, everything's going to be fine, just fine. JOSIE, GET IN HERE!!"

Forest told Olive that sometimes you want to be hidden, like he was in the

trees in the forest. But sometimes you want to be seen—like when he met Olive.

"I was scared," he told her, "but had to be brave. Now Olive has to be brave."

Olive thought about it. She looked around at all the faces of her classmates, waiting to hear her decision. They couldn't do *The Wizard of Oz* without a Wicked Witch. But Olive wasn't sure. Could she really do it?

Chapter 9

Olive knew the whole class was relying on her to save the show.

Forest looked at Olive. "You can do it. Forest be onstage, too. We are team."

That's exactly what Olive needed to hear. With Forest by her side, she felt stronger. "I'll do it!" she declared.

"Excellent!" said Mrs. Finn. "Now, hurry up and change. It's almost show time!"

"But what about *me*?" squeaked Josie.

"Oh, hmm," said Mrs. Finn. Then she brightened. "You can take Olive's part as a tree! The trees don't talk."

"No! I'm the star—"

"Shhhhh," Forest said to Josie. "Trees no talk."

Olive tried not to laugh, but failed. Josie glared at her but said nothing—for a change.

Forest watched as Olive put on her pointy witch's hat. "Forest like Olive's witch costume."

"Thanks, Forest," said Olive. "But your costume is even better. Those wings are so cool."

"Forest not actually fly," said Forest. "But Forest can flap!"

He flapped his arms.

"Ow!"

"Sorry, Darryl," said Forest.

"Break a leg!" Mrs. Finn told the cast.

"What?!" said Forest.

"Break a leg means 'good luck,'" explained Olive.

"Places, everyone!" Mrs. Finn called out.

All the students ran to their places on-stage if they were in the opening scene. As the curtain went up, Olive and all her classmates felt a rush of excitement in the air.

Celine Filibuster, in the role of Dorothy, took center stage, spouting her lines about her dreams and wishes to see a world beyond the farm. Meanwhile, in the wings, the rest of the cast gathered offstage to watch. All ready in her Wicked Witch out-fit, Olive joined them, along with Forest, eagerly waiting their turns to go onstage. She could just make out her dad, brother, and Gam Gam sitting in the audience, but it was hard to see with so many kids

crowding in the wings. They were going to be so surprised!

As Dorothy's scene finished, Olive turned to whisper something to Forest. But he wasn't there. She looked on the other side and around the crowd of kids. No luck. She looked backstage and near the makeup tables, but Forest wasn't there, either. A sinking feeling came over Olive. She looked up.

Yep, there he is, she thought, shaking her head.

Forest was twenty feet in the air, holding on to the rope that operated the curtain.

"Forest!" Olive said in her loudest whisper. "What are you doing up there?!"

"Forest not see down there!" he whispered back. "Too many kids!"

"Ugh!" said Olive. "You have to come down before someone sees you!"

Forest began to climb down, but pulled on the wrong rope, causing a backdrop of a huge tornado to drop down behind Dorothy.

Mrs. Finn gasped. Olive heard chuckles from the audience—the tornado

wasn't supposed to show up for five more minutes.

The rope Forest was holding on to went slack, and Forest, in his flying-monkey costume, fell in front of the back-drop, swinging across it—in full view of the audience! He let go, rolled when he hit the floor, and scampered off the stage.

Mrs. Finn grabbed the rope and pulled, hoisting up the tornado backdrop.

"Boy," said Dorothy onstage, "the weather here in Kansas sure does come and go real fast. And that was the funniest-looking crow I ever did see."

The audience chuckled again, and the play continued.

Finally, it was time for Olive's first scene onstage. She was still nervous but told herself to be brave, speak up, and be wicked! Darryl released a puff of smoke from a special machine onto the stage, and Olive walked into it. When she came out the other side on the stage, it looked as if she appeared by magic. The bright lights blinded her, and she realized it was silent. Everyone was waiting for her to speak. Suddenly, she wasn't scared. It was as if Olive had entered the smoke, but the Wicked Witch had come out of it. She pointed to Dorothy, who stood at the beginning of the yellow brick road.

"You horrid little girl!" she hissed. "You dare to wear my sister's slippers! Those belong to me!"

Celine Filibuster as Dorothy looked genuinely scared for a moment. She hadn't expected that from Olive.

"But the Good Witch of the East said not to give them to you," said Dorothy.

"They will be mine!" promised the witch. "Whether you're alive or dead!" With a cackle and another puff of smoke, she vanished.

Backstage, Mrs. Finn gave her a big hug. "Excellent job, Olive! My goodness, who would've known you had it in you?"

"Somebody had an idea," said Olive, looking over at Forest and winking.

"Glad to hear it," said Mrs. Finn. "Now, all the trees get out onstage! Yes, Josie, you, too. Remember trees don't look pouty. Just get out there."

Josie stomped onto the stage, apparently deciding to be a Scowling Willow.

As the show went on, Olive remembered every single one of her lines, and,

shockingly, began to enjoy herself onstage. But more importantly, Forest remembered what to do—and what *not* to do!

Soon it was time for the Wicked Witch's big finale with Dorothy. Olive took her place onstage, with Forest next to her. They faced Dorothy and her friends. The curtain rose and the lights came on, shining on the witch's lair,

adorned with gargoyles, black cauldrons, and books of spells.

Olive began to recite her lines.

"You fools!" cried the witch. Dorothy and her friends cowered. "I saw you every step of the way. Come to rescue your sweet little Dorothy? Well, instead, you'll share her fate." The witch raised her arms, ready to cast an evil spell.

Unfortunately, Forest had been standing a little too close to Olive during her speech, and when she raised her arms, she hit him with her broom. He took a step back, putting an arm out to balance. However, he'd forgotten his big monkey wings, which smacked into the crystal ball behind him. It dropped to the ground. It didn't break! Whew! But it did roll across the floor. . . .

"Eek!" said Forest. He chased after the rolling ball. Just before he caught it, he bumped into a table that held a bucket full of water. *Splash!* The bucket toppled and water went all over the floor.

The audience gasped. Dorothy and her friends gasped. They all knew that water was how the Wicked Witch was defeated.

But Olive didn't gasp. She didn't freak out. In fact, she handled herself like a true professional—she ad-libbed some new lines on the spot. She said, "Well, that was lucky. Good thing I didn't get wet. I'd just melt. Don't know why I keep that stuff around."

The audience laughed. From the wings, Mrs. Finn nodded with approval.

Back onstage, Forest knew he had to fix the water problem. That's when he spotted someone in the audience with a water bottle. He climbed down the front of the stage, stepped over some audience members, and onto the heads and shoulders of others.

"Oof!"

"Ouch!"

"Hey!!"

Forest plucked the water bottle out of the hands of a surprised mom, nodded his thanks, and returned to the stage. He dumped the water in the bucket and handed it to Dorothy.

"Throw!" he said to Dorothy.

Olive, as the witch, pointed at Forest and said, "You're fired, monkey!"

That got a huge laugh from the audience.

Then Olive did a most memorable melting scene that earned her a standing ovation when the curtain dropped.

Chapter 10

When the show was over and the curtain call was done, all the kids were flooded with energy. They hugged and congratulated one another.

Though she felt really good about her performance, Olive was still surprised that there were so many compliments bestowed upon her.

"Great job, Olive! Wow! That was awesome! You were the best Wicked Witch!"

"Thanks! Thank you!" she said, feeling a little embarrassed. She hoped Josie didn't hear that last comment!

But if she did, Josie didn't let on. "That wasn't too bad, Olive," Josie said.

"Thanks," said Olive. "You were a, uh, great tree."

Josie arched an eyebrow at Olive but smiled.

Olive turned to Forest. He was trying to get out of his costume, but he couldn't reach the zipper. Instead he just went around and around, like a dog chasing his tail.

"Congratulations, Forest," said Olive. "You did it! You did your first show!"

"WE did it," corrected Forest.

"Right," said Olive with a smile. "Maybe doing shows isn't so bad after all."

"What does Olive mean, 'shows'?" asked Forest. "We not done?"

Olive sighed. How was she going to explain there were three more shows?!

She smiled because she knew she'd figure out a way. Besides, with Forest as her right-hand monkey—and friend—she realized she could do anything.

About the Author

Tara Zann can't imagine living in a place without tall trees. Just like Forest, she has a spirit of adventure, though she might use a zip line instead of swinging from tree to tree on a long, dangling vine. She has no official pets, but dozens of creatures tend to stop by her backyard treehouse on a regular basis.

Read ALL the books in the WILD CHILD series!

Read on for
a sneak peek at
Forest's First Home!

Right in front of Olive was a boy who looked about her age. He was covered in a layer of dirt and was wearing a pair of shorts that looked to be made of leaves, mud, and who knows what else. His hair was messy and ragged, and appeared to have parts of an actual bird's nest in it. His green eyes shone wide and curious. Before Olive could say anything, the boy

scampered up the closest tree and onto a high branch.

"Wait!" called Olive.

The boy stopped and peered down at her. Olive looked up. She smiled. He smiled back. A tiny bird poked its head out of the boy's hair, let loose an irritated chirp, and flew off.

"Please come back," she said shyly.

Rather than climb down, the boy

grasped a vine and swung through the air. Olive gasped as he let go, flipped backward, and landed perfectly in front of her. *Who is this boy?* Olive had never seen anything like his acrobatics! Speechless, Olive began to clap. The boy seemed surprised by this but immediately started to clap, too.

"I'm Olive," she said, pointing to herself. "What's your name?"

"Forest," replied the boy.